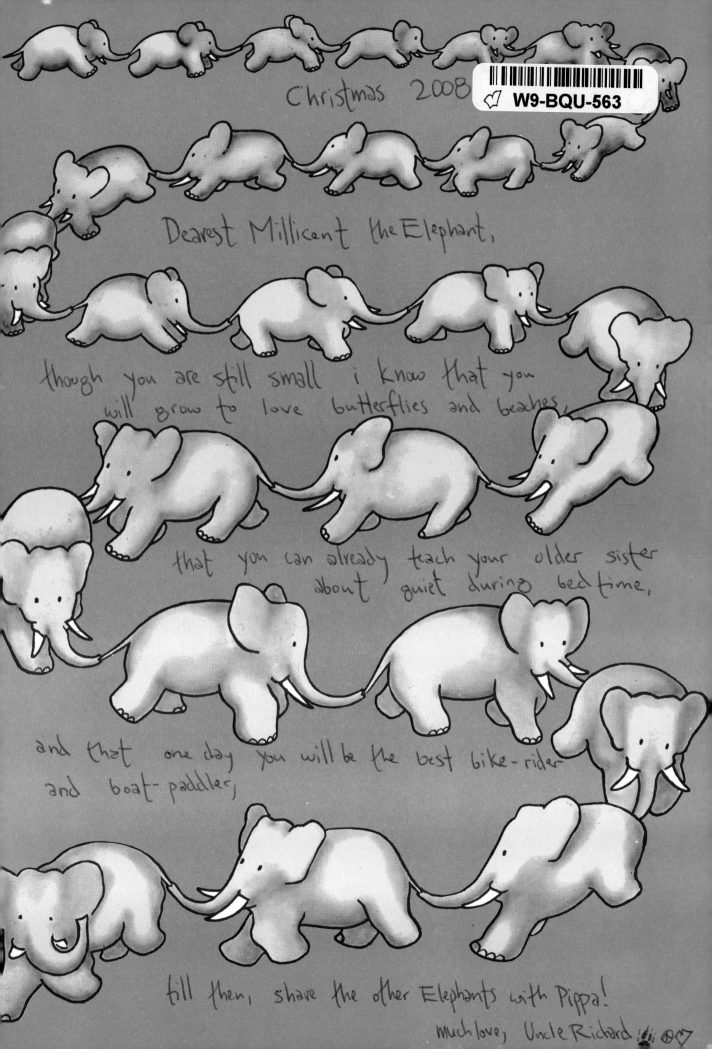

Christmas 2008

Dearest Millicent the Elephant,

though you are still small i know that you will grow to love butterflies and beaches,

that you can already teach your older sister about quiet during bedtime,

and that one day you will be the best bike-rider and boat-paddler;

till then, share the other Elephants with Pippa!

Much love, Uncle Richard

LAURENT DE BRUNHOFF

BABAR
and the
PROFESSOR

Translated from the French by MERLE HAAS
RANDOM HOUSE, INC. NEW YORK

The Babar Books

This title was originally cataloged by the Library of Congress as follows: Brunhoff, Laurent de, 1925–   Babar and the professor. Translated from the French by Merle Haas. New York, Random House [1957]   40 p. illus. 32 cm. Translation of Babar et le professeur Grifaton. I. Title.   PZ10.3.B7674Baa   57–11753   ISBN 0-394-80590-9   0-394-90590-3 (lib. bdg.)

King Babar and Queen Celeste are living happily in Celesteville, the city of the elephants, with their children Pom, Flora and Alexander, and their cousin Arthur. One day Babar gets a letter from his friend, the Old Lady.

"Children, listen to this," he says, and reads the letter aloud: "My dear Babar, I am homesick for you, and plan to visit you soon. My brother, Professor Grifaton, may come with me and bring his two grandchildren, Colin and Nadine. I look forward eagerly to seeing you again, and send you my warmest love."

"What wonderful news!" says Babar. "Hip hip hurrah!" cry all the children.

Here they are! Everyone is happy. Professor Grifaton is
deeply touched by their welcome: he has heard so much
about Babar and Celeste from his sister. Babar kisses

the Old Lady affectionately. Pom, Flora, and Alexander
are delighted to meet their new friends. And the car makes
a big hit with all the elephants.

The Old Lady goes to
her room. She quickly
unpacks her suitcases.
Then she calls in the
children. She has
brought presents for all
of them. Quick as a
flash, they tear off the

wrappings and open the boxes. The children are overjoyed and throw
themselves into the Old Lady's arms to hug and kiss her and thank her
for their presents. That night, at bedtime, no one feels sleepy. There is
so much to talk about; it is such fun to be together.

Suddenly, while rough-housing, Colin jumps on Pom's head and pulls his ear. Pom doesn't like this at all; he gets furious, catches the little fellow by the foot and whirls him around faster and faster.

"Stop that," cries Nadine. "Don't you dare hurt my brother!"

Flora and Alexander rush over to rescue Colin and throw pillows at Pom to make him stop.

All this noise brings Babar to the scene. "What's going on here? It is very late! Go to sleep now!" says he sternly.

The next day, Professor Grifaton takes the children to hunt butter- flies. He teaches them the names of the ones he catches in his butterfly net. Pom can't resist the temptation of blowing through his trunk on a beautiful yellow butterfly just as the Professor was about to catch it in his net. He is very much annoyed, but Colin thinks it's funny.

After their walk, the children go to the Professor's room. He shows them his butterfly case.

"You see," he explains to Pom, "it is made of plastic and can be taken apart and folded up when not in use. The little holes along the side let the air in."

Colin, sprawled on the rug, is looking at a picture book of butterflies. Arthur is admiring the microscope on the desk, but doesn't dare touch it.

All of a sudden, Nadine, who had not come back home with the others, calls to them through the window: "Alexander! Pom! Come quick! Come quick! I've just made a wonderful discovery!"

Nadine leads them to the entrance of a cave which is almost completely hidden behind tree branches. In great excitement, they decide to turn it into a playhouse. Pom brings some big cushions loaned by the Old Lady. The playhouse must be made comfortable. They light the cave with lanterns and go to work.

When all is ready in the cave, the children invite Babar, Celeste and their friends to a tea party. With the help of the Old Lady, they prepare a fine feast with lots of cakes. Arthur, the greedy little fellow, takes a whole plate of eclairs all for himself!

Babar, Celeste, and the Old Lady are left alone for a few minutes.
Then they see the children come back disguised in fancy costumes.

This was Nadine's idea for a big surprise. She found the costumes in a storeroom of a building used for the Fair at Celesteville!

Alexander goes to a tunnel leading from their playhouse to change his costume. While there he has a mischievous idea. "How about exploring to see where this tunnel goes?" he says to himself. He grabs a lantern and advances cautiously. After many twists and turns, the tunnel comes to an end in front of a big hole. Alexander leans over

to get a closer look.
He tries to see what is at the
bottom. Crash! He slips, rolls
over and tumbles into the hole. The
lantern is broken and it is pitch-black
down there. Alexander begins to cry and call
for help. . . . Finally, the others hear him and
come running with flashlights. Arthur slides down
into the hole to comfort him. Podular tosses a rope
to the little elephant and gently pulls him up.

After putting away their costumes, everybody gathers in King Babar's garden.

"This cave, it seems to me, is very interesting," says Professor Grifaton. "Don't you think, my dear Babar, that we might explore the tunnels leading from it?"

"What a splendid idea!" answers Babar. "We'll organize an expedition."

"Hurrah! Hurrah!" cries Arthur.

"Tomorrow I'll see that we have all the necessary equipment and tools," adds Cornelius.

"That will be fine," says King Babar, "and you, my dear Professor, should consult with my friend Podular, the sculptor. Exploring caves is his hobby."

Next day, Babar organizes a group to go down and explore the depths of the cave. This group, of course, includes Babar and Arthur, Podular the sculptor, Olur the mechanic, and Dr. Capoulosse who goes along in case he might be needed. Professor Grifaton and General Cornelius stay above ground, but are able to keep in touch with Babar by telephone. Having put on waterproof overalls and helmets with miners' lamps, the five elephants enter the cave while Colin and Nadine wave to them and cheer them on.

Having passed through Nadine's playhouse, they wander along zig-zag passages which become darker and darker. Babar and his friends suddenly find themselves in front of a strange-looking forest.

"Oh, what beautiful stalactites!" exclaims Podular.

Then, to add to the general excitement, the explorers discover a subterranean river!

Babar calls to Olur,
"Quickly, set up the tele-
phone! Hello, is that you,
Professor? We are in front
of a subterranean river!
Please ask Hatchibombotar,
the street cleaner, and
Pilophage, the army officer,
to lower the rubber rafts.
We're going to try to find
out where this river flows.
Do you want to come along?"

"Oh, yes, gladly," answers Grifaton. "I'll just hand over the telephone to Cornelius and I'll be right down."

"Arthur will go back to meet you at Nadine's rooms. He'll show
you the way," says Babar.

Soon the rubber rafts
arrive. Olur and his friend,
Hatchibombotar, blow them
up. When they get out of
breath, Arthur and Podular
change places with them.
Then the six rafts are
launched.

They glide along among the stalactites and the dim vaulted arches. All of a sudden an enormous statue appears out of the shadows. "It is the statue of the King of the Mammoths!" cries Arthur. "The Old Lady told us all about him at school!"

Thrilled by the discovery of this old hidden statue, Babar and his friends suddenly find themselves drifting out onto the lake at Celesteville. They are nearly blinded by the strong sunlight. There are many reeds in this part of the lake and only the fishermen and the pink flamingoes usually go there. Arthur would never have thought that Nadine's cave would lead this far....

After having notified Cornelius by telephone, the explorers paddle slowly back to Celesteville.

From their post at the entrance of the cave, all those who stayed with old General Cornelius come back cross-country on foot. The children can hardly wait to ask their friend Arthur all sorts of questions about the underground trip.

Next day the Professor has a long and mysterious talk with Babar.

Then he sits down at his desk and stays there many hours without raising his head.

In the afternoon, he walks along the garden paths completely lost in thought.

All at once, without saying a word to anyone, he rushes to his car, starts up the engine and is off.

The children have seen him and are puzzled. "What is he up to?" they ask one another.

He goes straight to see Hatchibombotar and tells him all about his great idea.

Hatchibombotar climbs up on the back step of the little car, and off he goes with the Professor.

Together they arrive at the harbor of Celesteville and stop at the shipyard. What's going on?

Professor Grifaton and Hatchibombotar have come to call on the commanding officer of the port.

"You see," says the Professor, "I thought it would be great fun if all the elephants could sail up the river by motor launch. This gave me the idea of building an excursion steamer which would make trips around the lake of Celesteville and stop off in front of the outlet of the river. There we'll have a landing platform and each passenger can choose his own raft to visit the cave. Here is the plan for the steamer."

"Great idea!" said the commanding officer. "Let's have a look at it."

EXCURSION STEAMER

Idea conceived and designed
by Professor Grifaton

PROPELLED BY ATOMIC ENGINES
WITH SIDE PADDLE–WHEELS

DIAGRAM

1. Captain's cabin
   and bridge
2. Dining room
3. Bar and Library
4. Ballroom
5. Kitchen
6. Refrigerator

7. Purser's office
8. Hospital
9. Photographer
10. Shop
11. Coatroom

12. Engine room
13. Hold
14. A Deck
15. B Deck
16. Paddle wheel

EXCURSION STEAMER
TOUR OF THE LAKE   20¢
FARE FOR THE CAVE   10¢
DEPARTURE TIME 2:30 P.M.

ICE CREAM

A little later, the excursion boat is ready for its first trip. "Your great idea has come true, Professor," says Babar. "All the ele-

phants are delighted." The siren blows. The crowd hurries over. The sailors prepare to cast off. But where are the children?

Arthur and his little friends have gone off for a ride on their bicycles.
Colin and Nadine are sitting together in the trailer behind Arthur.
When it is almost time for the excursion steamer to leave, the children
are still far away. "Hurry up! Hurry up! We'll be late!" All of a sudden
at a sharp turn, the trailer loses a wheel. Pom, who was right behind,
jams on his brake. Crash! Down they go with a bang.

Colin rolls over and over curled up like a ball and doesn't hurt himself. But big fat Pom is quite shaken up, and Nadine skins her knee. Flora gently blows on it to ease the pain, and Alexander tries to signal a passing car. Luckily, Olur, the mechanic, comes by. He helps them into his truck and drives them to the harbor of Celesteville.

"If only we get there in time," says Arthur, anxiously.

DEPARTURE TIME TOMORROW

①

Too late! The steamer has left, and the gate is closed until tomorrow.

②

A sailor, seeing them so disappointed, calls to them and says: "In five minutes

③

the excursion steamer will pass under the bridge. Run quickly! You can catch up with it there."

④

The children run as fast as their legs can carry them. They are on the bridge just in the nick of time.

⑤

Arthur leans over the railing and waves wildly at the steamer.

⑥

The Captain on the bridge sees them and gives the order to stop.

⑦

As soon as the boat stops, a rope ladder is thrown to them from the stern.

Upset but proud of their escapade, the children fling themselves into the arms of Babar and Celeste.

"Whatever happened to you?" asks Celeste. "Didn't I tell you that there wasn't enough time to go for a bicycle ride before the steamer sailed?"

Then Arthur explains the whole story of what happened to them. Afterwards he leans over the rail and watches the water flowing gently under the boat.

"What a delightful excursion!" the Old Lady says to her brother, Professor Grifaton. "How I love the lake of Celesteville!"

Arriving at the entrance to the cave and the subterranean river, the steamer draws up alongside the pier. The passengers land and choose a motorboat. Cornelius and the Old Lady are afraid of the dampness in the cave because of their rheumatism. They call to the others: "Good-bye! Be careful! Remember, no nonsense!"

"Choo choo! Let's go!" cries Arthur. Babar turns on his searchlight.

The searchlights illuminate the cave and make it

look enormous. Truly, it is the Palace of the Mammoths!

An hour later the steamer comes in sight of the harbor of Celesteville.

"Hurrah for the excursion boat! Hurrah for Professor Grifaton!" cry all the elephants crowded behind the railing. Everyone twists and turns to get the best view. The little ones climb up on their parents' shoulders and on top of the cars.

   "Tomorrow we'll get here bright and early to find a good place," one of them says. "I'll be the first."

   "No! I will!" says another.

That evening, at the Assembly Hall, Cornelius decorates Professor Grifaton as Benefactor of Celesteville, and pins a medal on his chest. The ceremony takes place in the presence of King Babar and Queen Celeste. The children, in their pajamas, watch the proceedings over television. The Old Lady is with them. They are all excited and applaud loudly.

Finally the day arrives when Professor Grifaton must return home. The vacation is over. After packing his bags, he and Colin and Nadine sadly say good-bye to all their friends. The Professor kisses his sister the Old Lady. Regretfully he says good-bye to Babar and Celeste. He and his grandchildren step into his car. All three are agreed that they must soon come back again to the country of the elephants.